THE WICKEDEST TEACHER IN THE WORLD

Chris Nicholls

Illustrated by
Jon Riley

I

When Alex suggested sending Mrs Thoroughgood's name up to *The Guinness Book of Records* to put under "Worst Teacher in the World", nearly everyone in the class was enthusiastic. Only Phil doubted the practicality of the idea.

"They wouldn't put it in," he said. "You have to give them some figures as well, to prove something."

"How about 'Number of children killed'?" retorted Alex.

Sensible Brenda was the only one who thought that Mrs Thoroughgood wasn't as bad as the others believed.

"It's only because Alex keeps saying so," she argued. "And that's only because he doesn't *like* her, which isn't the same as her being a bad teacher. Look at Miss Smalley—she's as nice as a Mars Bar, but she can't teach for toffee apples."

Plump, popular Brenda knew a thing or two about Mars Bars and toffee apples. She was an odd mixture, enjoyed for her mad outbursts of jollity, listened to because she also talked common sense, and feared for her everlasting hunger for food—anyone's food.

Alex's idea about "Number of children killed" was not quite as absurd as it sounds though, if you take into account the stories that went round—mostly started by Alex—about Mrs Thoroughgood's wickedness. While no one had actually seen her do anything incredibly awful, there were strange bits of evidence that did exist, if, like Alex, you wanted to put two and two together and make three thousand.

Take the case of little John Jones, for example. He had been a rather pathetic boy—one of those with a pale sunken face and an ever-running nose, that doesn't try to join in and isn't ever asked. He'd arrived unexpectedly in the class two weeks after last term began, and the only thing that had made people glad of his presence was the way he managed to attract so much of Mrs Thoroughgood's hatred so quickly. While he was there, she picked on him about ten times every lesson, for no apparent good reasons. But that meant ten pickings-on fewer to be shared among the others.

Then, after three weeks, little John Jones had disappeared as completely and suddenly as he'd arrived. No one dared to ask Mrs Thoroughgood what had happened to him, because you didn't ask her things like that for fear of getting your head bitten off. And since no one had bothered to ask him where he lived or who his parents were, no one could know where or why he'd gone. Therefore, said Alex, there could be only one explanation: "Mrs Thoroughgood did him in."

Alex's friends liked to discuss in revolting detail exactly *how* she'd done him in. Brenda's preferred to concentrate on the mysteries of the disappearance itself—how she'd threatened him with the point of her black umbrella, then bundled him into her car, covered his head with a rug, and whisked him off to her lonely house. All agreed that he must have been doing something stupid, like being near her car in the first place, to have got caught so easily.

And the car itself was another piece of the evidence against her, both because of the terrible threats she uttered to anyone who went near it, and because of the kind of car it was. It was big, powerful, brand-new, and extremely expensive, with chrome gadgets all over it, a dazzling display of coloured lights at the back, and all sorts of accessories like a sunroof, electric windows, and wipers everywhere. Those who had dared to creep near enough to peep inside swore that it not only had quadrophonic sound but a drinks cabinet and a television screen in the back as well.

Miss Smalley drove a clapped-out old Renault, small and dirty, with rust-holes. Even the Head only had a four-year-old Escort. No teacher possibly could, or should, have a car like Mrs Thoroughgood's unless they were getting a lot of extra money from something else. Alex had seen enough television to know that only people who were already rich or who were crooks drove cars like that—and why should Mrs Thoroughgood be already rich? Therefore she was a crook.

Then there was also the fact that she was mad on computers. Normally you had to forgive teachers for going on at you about some pet hobby they were mad on, such as football or music or nature rambles. With Mrs Thoroughgood everyone was so suspicious already that they went round saying things like, "Yes, but why *computers*? What does she *use* them for?"

To Alex, the answer was simple. At her lonely house, she had a huge central computer which she used to control a vast network of criminal activities. She also used it to keep tabs on the children in her class. How else could she know so brilliantly—as she always seemed to— exactly what they'd done and even what they were going to do next?

"What about the time I brought that fantastic variety pack of bubble gums to school that my uncle in America sent me?" Alex ticked off the points against Mrs Thoroughgood on his fingers:

"*First* she said, 'What are you hiding?' the moment I came in the classroom.

"*Then* when I said, 'Nothing' she said, 'We'll see', as if she knew for sure.

"*Then* I hid it in Brenda's tray, and a bit later she asked to see Brenda's tray and found it.

"*Then*, instead of blaming Brenda, she said, 'I think this is yours, Alex.'

"*So*—" Alex clinched his argument— "the point is, she knew I'd had a parcel from America, didn't she? Else how could she have done all that? And the reason she knew was because it all goes down on that computer of hers. I'll bet it's got a zillion K memory, and it controls secret spy-cameras everywhere."

"She might just have guessed," said Phil, who was Alex's best friend for that week. He didn't really want to argue, because being Alex's best friend was the very best and most exciting thing to be— short of being Alex himself. But even so, you had to show a bit of independence.

"Huh!" said Alex. "No one's that good a guesser. I tell you she *knows*, man." He decided he wouldn't bother having Phil as a best friend any more, if Phil was going to start getting uppity.

II

Away in her lonely house, Mrs Thoroughgood sat at the console of her vast computer feeling irritated and dissatisfied. Things were not going very well with her Empire of Crime, nor with her class. For example, her hidden microphones and cameras were picking up conversations among the children that made it pretty clear they were on to her—they seemed to know so many of her secrets already. But she couldn't for the life of her think *how* they knew.

Had it perhaps been that little spy-child, John Jones? She'd known he must be a spy the moment she caught him snooping furtively round her car. But although he'd certainly seen the monitor screen in the back, he'd surely had no opportunity to get a message to the rest of the class, for she'd bundled him straight into the back, covered his head with a rug, and once he was safely here, the robots had dealt with him.

For the hundredth time since it had happened she checked, typing in J-O-H-N J-O-N-E-S on the keyboard in front of her. Screen 12 flashed the answer immediately:

JONES, JOHN
BORN 08.1.80
LIQUIDATED 15.2.90

As with every time she ran this check, she let out a huge sigh of relief. There was no mistake, and no chance at all that he could have talked.

So it must be someone else. Her mind immediately produced the name "Alex". She didn't trust that Alex at all. He was too bright, too sure of himself, too cunning. He seemed to believe he could outwit her, and although he couldn't, there was danger in his even thinking so. She was just about to run a visual check on him when Screen 7 suddenly flared into life with the words:

URGENT MESSAGE
URGENT MESSAGE
URGENT MESSAGE

Her finger stabbed the "Receive" key, and a worried-looking face replaced the words on the screen:

"Barclay, from Hong Kong," it said.

"What's your problem, Barclay?" snapped Mrs Thoroughgood.

"The diamond operation. I don't know what went wrong, but the cops were waiting for our agent when he tried to smuggle them through customs. Someone must have squealed."

"Barclay, I don't pay you to hand me your problems. You're there to sort them out. Find out who squealed and have him or her liquidated. Right?"

"Yes, Mrs Thoroughgood. Right."

Screen 7 went blank again.

Was it possible, mused Mrs Thoroughgood, was it possible that this Alex knew far more about her organisation than the fact that it existed? Could he, for example, conceivably know anything about the Hong Kong diamond operation? Could he know enough to have got her agent arrested? Surely not. But she'd better run that check *now*.

She rapidly typed in instructions for Screen 18 to display what spy-camera No. 583 was showing. There was a tiny pause, while the computer lumberingly worked it out, then Screen 18 lit up.

Alex's bedroom. He wasn't in it, which meant that he could be up to all sorts of no-good somewhere—perhaps out of range of any of her cameras. Better to have a quick look round his room before trying to locate him, in case he'd left anything at all revealing. She instructed the camera to rotate.

The room was a disgusting mess; that was the most obvious fact about it—the bed not made, clothes all over the floor mixed up with toys and bits of toys, a poster half hanging off the wall. She couldn't begin to imagine how anyone so incapable of organising his own bedroom would dare to challenge her almost perfectly organised network.

Was that perhaps a clue, over on his chest of drawers? A transmitter? She zoomed in on it, but close up it turned out to be nothing more than a cheap cassette player. Next to it was something that could be a bit more promising, but this was only a cheap plastic plane kit—a quarter done, bits missing (probably somewhere in that muck on the floor) and glue oozing out all over the chest of drawers because he hadn't put the top back on the tube.

She angrily punched at the keyboard again, and screen after screen came to life as she searched urgently for him:

The living-room in Alex's house—
empty.

Phil's bedroom—
deserted.

The park—
lots of people, but not Alex.

Swimming baths—
the same.

Several streets, one after another—
nothing.

More houses of children in her class—
nothing.

The classroom—
deserted, of course, on a Saturday.

Now furious, Mrs Thoroughgood extinguished all the screens with one stab of her finger. Where was Alex? And what was he planning?

III

Alex was actually quite a long way off, with Phil. His parents had decided that a day trip to the sea would be a good idea on such a beautiful May Saturday. Alex had persuaded them to let him bring Phil, because even though he was going to ditch Phil as best friend, he hadn't yet found anyone to replace him. Having Phil along was far better than having nobody at all to listen to him.

They left Alex's parents huddled against a stone wall, out of the cold wind, and began to walk along the beach. Phil wanted to build something in sand, or race waves, or chuck stones, but Alex obviously wanted to walk and talk. So they walked, and Alex talked.

"The key to it all is what happened to John Jones. If we could find that out for sure, we'd probably be able to get at her whole system."

"What system?" Phil asked dutifully.

"Aw, come on, man. It stands to reason she's not just a teacher. None of the other teachers has a car like hers. None of the others are nutty about computers like she is. And none of them manage to get a class as quiet as she gets ours. I tell you, she's got some way of doing it, and she just liquidates anyone who gets in her way."

"If you think that's what happened to John Jones, why don't you go and tell the police?" Phil was bored. He'd heard it all

before, and he hated wasting a day by the sea hearing it all again.

Alex stared back at him with icy distaste. Next week he'd have a very different best friend—a girl, even. Yes, why not a girl? It sounded quite big and tough to have a girl-friend actually—as though you didn't need the support of another lad.

"The police!" he scoffed. "What bog did you crawl out of, man? As if they'd believe a schoolboy telling fantastic stories about his class teacher."

Phil simply couldn't cope with Alex's ability to make almost anything part of his game. It felt to him as if Alex was always changing the rules to suit himself.

"Get lost," he muttered, wondering why anyone—especially him—should want to be Alex's best friend.

"Find your own way home, then!" Alex turned and marched off back towards his parents.

Phil wasn't going to be bullied by a cheap trick like that. Even if Alex might be prepared to leave him stranded there, his parents wouldn't. Would they? No, they wouldn't. Nevertheless, he ran after Alex just in case there should be any mistake.

"Go on!" Phil taunted. "If you're so sure she's all those things you keep inventing, why don't you find out? Why don't you follow her to her house and find out?"

Alex turned to glare back. "That's just what I'm going to do. And I'm going to do it without *your* help."

They spent the rest of the day playing quite happily together, making things with sand, racing waves, and chucking stones.

IV

Spying on someone who drives a very fast car, when all you've got is an old BMX with a mud-caked chain, is not that easy. But Alex was determined to show Phil, and he was also determined to establish himself in the eyes of his new best friend, Brenda. Not that she knew she was his best friend. He hadn't told her yet—only because he wasn't quite *sure*, and not because he didn't dare.

On the Monday, after school, he was ready waiting on his bike. When Mrs Thoroughgood's car appeared, he hared after it, keeping at a safe distance, and lost

her where the street the school was in joined the main road. He saw her turn left at the junction, but by the time he got there, she was out of sight. Not too brilliant as a first effort, Alex reflected, considering that the chase couldn't have covered more than a hundred metres altogether.

So on the Tuesday, he waited at the junction and hared after her along the main road till she was too far ahead to be seen.

On the Wednesday, he positioned himself on the main road, at the point where he'd last seen her, but she never appeared at all. He got fed up with waiting, and went home.

Things weren't going too well with Brenda either. She was so proper, so well-behaved, so slow and deliberate, and always so hungry. She clearly didn't think it quite decent to be seen to be Alex's best friend (if indeed she was), but above all she resented the kind of sharing that best friends went in for. If she had a bag of crisps she wanted it all to herself; if Alex had a bag of crisps, she wanted that all to herself as well.

In fact, Alex was beginning to wonder if she wasn't a dead loss. The only thing that could possibly account for her popularity was that she also had this streak of incredible jollity. You only had to bat your eyelids at her to make her giggle, and if you went on doing it, she dissolved into hysterics and was practically rolling on the floor in a few seconds. Alex, who rarely smiled and never giggled, because he had serious things on his mind, began to think she wasn't his type at all.

Thursday was a good day. He stuck with Brenda through all the breaks, and at least it looked as if they were best friends, and at least everyone else—girls *and* boys—was going round discontented as anything about it. And after school Mrs Thoroughgood's car did appear at the point where it hadn't on Wednesday, and he not only saw where she turned off the main road, but managed to catch up with her when she stopped to post a letter.

Then it was only a short ride till the car turned in at the gate of a largish and definitely posh house. It wasn't exactly a lonely house, but it was a detached one— really quite detached. And it was a good deal posher than any ordinary teacher ought to have. What was more, there was already another expensive car parked in the drive, looking as if it belonged—a huge, grey car—a Mercedes, surely.

Alex took it all in, laying his plans, while she got out of her car and went into the house. He was certain she hadn't seen him. Nor could he be in any danger from the spy-cameras he knew must be watching the area in front of the house, until she could get to her console. But the moment the front door slammed behind her, he knew he could be in awful danger, and he took off for home.

Brenda was not at all impressed when he told her about it on Friday—either by Alex's sleuthing powers or by the danger he might have been in. She still held on to her view that Mrs Thoroughgood was not a bad person; just not a very nice one. She thought Alex's tales about computers and spy-cameras were daft. Alex began to hate the way she wouldn't be bossed about and told what to think. He decided to ditch her next week.

Brenda, however, had no idea that she was going to be ditched, because she never considered she'd been taken up in the first place. As far as she was concerned, it was quite pleasant having Alex hanging around her, giving her all his crisps, but that didn't mean *she* had to do anything or be anything in particular.

V

Mrs Thoroughgood had realised what Alex was up to, of course. You don't get to the top of the underworld without being able to spot a small boy on a bike, following your car day after day, and hanging around outside your house—nor without being able to conceal the fact that you've spotted him. The only question was what to do about him.

She could just have him liquidated by the robots. On the face of it, that would be simplest. Except that two disappearances in one year from the same class—her class—might begin to attract too much attention, and attention was the last thing she wanted at the moment, with one of the most important operations she'd ever planned coming up. In any case, how much might Alex have already said to the others in the class, to make them suspect her straight away if he did disappear?

Once this operation was over, she wouldn't need to bother about Alex—or about anyone. She would have everyone so firmly under her thumb that they could say what they liked, and if they did happen to annoy her, one flick of a switch and the robots would see to them...

But it was no good day-dreaming about the future. The point was that right now Alex was a menace, who had either to be stopped completely or at least slowed down somehow.

That last phrase popping into her mind gave her the idea she'd been searching for. He could literally be slowed down. His transport could be not so much immobilised as slightly disabled—just enough to put him off, but not enough to confirm any of his suspicions or give him any clear evidence.

She set to work at once on the keyboard, programming a robot to carry out the complicated instruction overnight. It was a long way to Alex's house, and there was the risk that the robot might be seen on the way there or back. Both the route and the time had to be carefully worked out.

A flashing on Screen 7 distracted her. She pressed a key, and Barclay's face appeared, looking even more worried.

"You're interrupting me, Barclay. What have you got to report? Make it quick."

"We bribed a detective to get the source of the leak, Mrs Thoroughgood. But it seems it wasn't from here at all. It came from England, and it was just an anonymous call to the police here."

"Didn't they trace it?"

"All this detective knew was that it came from a phone box somewhere in your area. I can't handle it from this end, Mrs Thoroughgood."

"Don't you tell me what you can and can't do, Barclay. *I'll* decide that."

"What shall I do about the agent they arrested, Mrs Thoroughgood?"

"Break him out of gaol, you fool. I don't care if you have to bribe the whole Hong Kong police force and the prison service as well, but get him out—before he talks. Just get it *done*."

She switched him off before he even had time to mouth a reply, and returned to programming the robot. A phone box somewhere in this area! It could only be Alex: no one else round here had even the beginnings of enough imagination to interfere in the Hong Kong operation. Which made her present task all the more urgent.

She started tapping frantically at the keys, growing more and more frenzied as the image of Alex's smug little face became stronger and stronger in her mind.

VI

In spite of the slow puncture his bike seemed to have developed overnight, after borrowing a pump from a neighbour, Alex managed to fulfil his plan of watching Mrs Thoroughgood's house all Saturday morning.

Not that there was a lot to watch. Mrs Thoroughgood's car and the Mercedes were both there in the drive again. At 10.26 Mrs Thoroughgood went off in her car, and six minutes later a bald-headed man came out and began to mow the front lawn. Alex couldn't guess where she might have gone, but the bald-headed man was clearly someone high up in her organisation, whose duty was to keep an eye on the front of the house while she was out. He might perhaps be her personal bodyguard, or one of her trusted "heavies". Certainly he looked quite heavy, even if too much of his heaviness was fat.

It was not easy to keep a good watch without being seen. Pretending to inspect his puncture for the fourteenth time, Alex cursed all his ex-friends and classmates for being so dull. With a mate here, they could easily have cycled up and down the road, past the house, quite realistically pretending to play. All they'd have had to do was to make sure Mrs Thoroughgood didn't recognise them.

At one point, he even caught himself thinking, "If only Phil was here!" He did his best to dismiss the thought sharply, because there was no way he was going crawling back to Phil, and anyway Phil wouldn't have come.

He tried replacing it with, "If only Brenda was here!" but that was worse still. Even if he'd dared suggest it to her, and if she'd agreed, and if she had a bike (which she probably didn't) and if she could ride it (which she probably couldn't)—even then she'd only want to do something stupid, like stand around in full view of Mrs Thoroughgood, so she could say, "Good morning" to her. Or else she'd be in helpless giggles on the pavement at the sight of that heavy, bald-headed man desperately trying to stop his motor mower from crashing into the flower beds, and failing.

In any case he'd decided to ditch Brenda, but this too was a worry. She hadn't really given him any room to use his preferred method of ditching—to go up to her and say in a frank and serious way, "I'm afraid I don't want you as my best friend any more, Brenda". He was afraid she'd only laugh and walk away instead of looking downcast and a bit shaken, as all the others had (all except Phil, who'd said, "That's good, because I was just going to say the same to you.").

These rather depressing thoughts were interrupted by the return of Mrs Thoroughgood's car, which made it necessary to carry out another long examination of his tyre to hide his face. He supposed that she'd been out to visit one of her local hit-men—or possibly even to his own house to see if she could run him down with her car—so it was something of a disappointment to squint cautiously up and see her emerge with carrier-bags full of shopping and take them into her house.

She came out of the house again almost immediately, holding a newspaper she'd obviously just bought. She walked across the lawn to where the bald-headed man was still fighting with the mower, and showed him something in it. Alex strained hard to see, but from where he was, on the far side of the road, all he could make out was that it was probably the local paper, and that she was pointing to something on the front page. He had to duck his head down more than once to avoid his face being seen. The tyre really was getting quite dangerously flat.

The moment she'd gone indoors, he was off like a flash—never mind the tyre— before she could get to her console and zoom one of those cameras in on him. Half way along the main road the back wheel started bumping and he cursed his bad luck—now he'd have to push the stupid thing the rest of the way, and there'd be no chance of going back to resume his surveillance in the afternoon.

One thing he did manage to do on his way home, however, was to nip into the local newsagent's. There was no need even to buy a copy of the paper, because the front page was almost completely taken up with only one story, and there it was, spread out on the counter:

The Gazette

PRIME MINISTER'S SURPRISE VISIT

Nuclear power site to get top level vetting

WIN A METR
See p.4

At first Alex couldn't make much of it. He supposed there was no reason why Mrs Thoroughgood shouldn't be interested in other things, as well as her Empire of Crime—things like prime ministers and nuclear power stations and such. Though he couldn't see why she should bother showing it to her bodyguard.

Then the answer burst upon him. Of course, of course, of course! For reasons he couldn't begin to understand, she was planning to have the Prime Minister assassinated on the day of the visit!

VII

If you happen to hold important information, known only to yourself, that your class teacher is planning to assassinate the Prime Minister quite soon, and if you haven't a jot of evidence to back it up, and if you know that no one will believe you anyway, then you have problems. Alex spent the rest of Saturday wrestling with them.

What was needed urgently, of course, was hard evidence. He was so determined to get some that he even spent a lot of the afternoon wrestling with his back tyre, so as to be fully mobile the next day. His father was so astonished at not being called in to help (i.e. do it all, while Alex watched) that he went and bought Alex a new pump.

By Sunday morning Alex had decided what to do. It was a fine morning, and his parents were only staying at home doing gardening, but there was just a chance that Mrs Thoroughgood and her bodyguard would take advantage of it by going out for the day, or at least part of it. Immediately after breakfast he biked out to her house.

It looked encouragingly deserted when he arrived, but of course it needed checking out very thoroughly. He parked his bike further up the road, and walked past her house several times, always shielding his face with his nearside hand so as to prevent recognition via the spy-cameras. After all, she might well, even now, be at her console, watching the whole scene and chuckling evilly to herself.

Neither her car nor the Mercedes were out at the front, he noted. But then they could both be in the garage. Or she might have gone out, but only somewhere close, like to get a paper or to church, and she might be back any moment. There seemed no way of telling.

Then he had a stroke of luck. A boy delivering Sunday papers suddenly appeared as if from nowhere, went skidding up Mrs Thoroughgood's drive, then still sitting on his bike, propping himself up with one hand on the wall, gave a long, hard ring at her bell. Getting no reply, he rapped with the knocker. Then he tried clattering the letter-box flap. Only when it was quite clear that no one was coming to answer, did he shove the paper through the door.

Alex knew it wasn't cast-iron proof she was out, but he also knew he couldn't hope for anything better. It was time to make his move. After all, if she did suddenly arrive back, he'd hear the car and be able to hide while she got out, and then make a dash the moment the front door closed behind her—before she could get to her console.

It still needed a lot of courage to actually do it, but Alex hadn't got to his powerful position in the class without having plenty of that. On his next patrol past, he turned sharply and marched boldly up the drive, as if he was just another newspaper boy. When he got to the house, he walked quickly along the front to the corner, then slipped down the side.

Here, trees and bushes hid him from the road, and it was safe to begin his investigation. He didn't have far to investigate. He'd expected somehow to have to find a way down into the cellar, or up into an attic, but there, in the very first room he peered into, was the console—a fair-sized screen with a great big keyboard in front of it. Far from being concealed, it faced the window he was looking through, even resting on a table that looked very much like an ordinary dining-room table.

It certainly wasn't as he'd imagined it would be. He realised that, in fact, one screen would be enough, and you didn't actually need lots; it was just that when they showed that sort of set-up in films, they always did have lots. The keyboard really was quite big, though—well, it was a lot bigger than any of the ones they had at school—well, it was a *bit* bigger.

On the other hand, he wasn't too sure of its value as evidence. It certainly wasn't the kind of thing that would interest the police, and, therefore, there was a good chance that it wouldn't impress any of his mates either. He though of Phil's likely reaction.

"So she's got a blah-blah-blah computer," Phil would say (he would know the make). "So what?"

And as for the idea of trying to impress Brenda with it . . . Alex shuddered.

What clinched the whole thing for Alex, however, was something he hadn't noticed earlier. On the table, right beside the keyboard, was the newspaper he'd seen her with yesterday. And *the* headline was face up too—he could even see the words "SURPRISE VISIT". Obviously she had been sending messages about it through her network, or else perhaps programming instructions for someone. Even that, he knew, was not conclusive evidence. People never took any notice till it was too late to do any good, or unless it was so glaring they couldn't avoid noticing it.

He snooped a bit further—on round the back of the house, where there was just a sun-lounge, a patio, quite a decent-sized garden. There was nothing of the kind he wanted—no shed big enough to hold many robots, no little gravestone marked "John Jones", not even any old cardboard boxes with Hong Kong stamps on them.

He came to a decision. Mrs
Thoroughgood had obviously been
expecting him, and she'd managed to make
the whole set-up appear completely
innocent. There was therefore no point in
continuing to investigate here. The only
plan of action open to him was to catch her
in the very act of trying to assassinate the
Prime Minister. That way he'd save the
country and expose Mrs Thoroughgood at
the same time. He'd be a double hero, and
Phil and Brenda could go and take running
jumps.

VIII

From the real console in her cellar, Mrs Thoroughgood watched every move Alex made with huge satisfaction. She'd particularly enjoyed getting a close-up of his face while he was peering in through the dining-room window—the way his pleased expression, when he caught sight of her old home computer, had changed to one of doubt. Then his futile little snoop round the back. What was he expecting to find? Boxes marked "Hong Kong Diamonds. Fragile. With Care."?

At the same time, it had been careless of her to leave that newspaper so close to the old computer. Would he make the connection? Surely he was far too stupid ever to work out what she had in mind—though if he had been the one who'd foiled the Hong Kong operation, she couldn't rely on that. She would have to continue to keep a sharp watch on him.

She pressed a switch and spoke into a microphone. "Villansky. Come here, to the control room."

A few seconds later, there was a knock at the door and the bald-headed man entered.

"Has the equipment come?" she asked him.

"Just arrived, Mrs Thoroughgood." He spoke with a heavy foreign accent.

"Let's see it, then. Fetch it."

He went out, and reappeared in a few moments with a long cardboard box cradled in his arms. He held it while Mrs Thoroughgood took off the lid and folded back the wrappings inside. She took out of it a slender, black umbrella, neatly rolled.

"This looks excellent, Villansky. They've done a good job. Is it silenced?"

"Yes, Mrs Thoroughgood. They say so."

"Good. Get it ready." She handed the umbrella to Villansky, who fiddled around with it, inserted something in the handle, then passed it back to her.

"Now go and stand over there, and hold the box in the air."

Looking very nervous, Villansky picked up the box the umbrella had come in, and walked over to the other side of the room. Then he turned to face Mrs Thoroughgood, stretching the hand with the box in it high in the air. He seemed to be trying to get it as far away from himself as he possibly could.

Mrs Thoroughgood stood up, holding the umbrella very naturally, as if she was standing on some street corner chatting to a friend. Opposite her Villansky quivered, so that the box trembled above him.

Quite slowly—as though she was casually pointing out to her friend some object of interest—Mrs Thoroughgood raised the tip of the umbrella in the direction of the box. There was a sudden little pphtt! sound, the box gave a twitch, and a small lump of plaster fell out of the wall directly behind it.

Villansky lowered his arm with a huge sigh of relief, inspected the box, and brought it over to her. There was a neat, round hole right in the middle of it.

"It's good," she said, inspecting the hole and nodding with satisfaction.

"*You're* good," returned Villansky.

"The best, Villansky, the best. That's why I'm not trusting this baby to anyone else." She patted the handle of the umbrella. "This is one job I'm going to do myself, and it's going to be done right."

"You're putting yourself at risk, Mrs Thoroughgood," Villansky ventured.

"What risk? A harmless teacher with a class of silly kids? They won't even begin to think of suspecting me."

"And where will you want me, Mrs Thoroughgood?"

"Right beside me. All the time. If anything does go wrong, which it won't, you take this—" she lifted the umbrella—

"and you get away to your car in the confusion. Then you're on your own. That's what you're paid for."

"Yes, Mrs Thoroughgood."

"And one other thing. Before it happens, you make sure I'm not going to be jostled by anyone. You screen me from those nauseating little kids—especially one of 'em."

"Which one's that?"

"The one they call Alex. I don't think he knows anything, but he's got a nasty, suspicious mind. Ten to one he'll be snooping around near me just to try and be a nuisance."

"You leave him to me, Mrs Thoroughgood."

"I will, Villansky. Once it's all over and I've got a real grip on things, we'll be able to do what we want with him. You'll enjoy that, won't you Villansky?"

"Oh, I will, Mrs Thoroughgood. I *will*."

IX

"Now class, I want you to listen very carefully. If any child is stupid enough to say they don't understand the arrangements after I've finished, I shall explain them personally to that child after school.

"Next Wednesday—that's *Wednesday*, the twenty-eighth of May—a most important visitor is coming to the town. Does anyone know who it is?"

"Would it be the Mayor, Mrs Thoroughgood?" Sweet Mary Clough had blurted it out even before other hands had shot up.

Mrs Thoroughgood strode over to where Mary Clough was sitting, and leaned over her menacingly. "To be as silly as you are, Mary Clough, is bad enough. To be rude as well as silly is pathetic. I want neither calling out nor imbecilic answers in this classroom. How *could* the visitor be the Mayor? No one is witless enough to talk about the Mayor being a "visitor" to his own town—not even me, Mary Clough. Yes, Brenda?"

"It's the Prime Minister, Mrs Thoroughgood."

"Of course it is. The Prime Minister is not only coming to the town, but will be passing along the main road, only a hundred or so metres from this school. I have decided that this class will join with the others in going to watch them pass by—not because you deserve it but just so you can say I gave you the opportunity to see your Prime Minister.

"Now these are the arrangements. There will be an extended break until ten past eleven. After that, you will come back into the classroom and from here you will be taken to assemble on the front playground. The Prime Minister is due to pass the end of this street at about a quarter to twelve.

Now, does anyone not understand, and are there any questions? Yes, David?"

"What if it's raining, Mrs Thorough-good?"

"Well, that's why I'm warning you, isn't it, you silly boy? We shall go whether it's raining or not. Those of you who are normally so thoughtless as not to bring macs or anoraks had better think again. Nobody, however bedraggled they get, will be allowed one inch of shelter under my umbrella."

Alex stared transfixed, as she indicated her slender, black, rolled umbrella leaning against the end of the radiator. That wasn't, of course, the actual one—the one she'd tried out in her cellar. But that "special" umbrella would be an exact replica of this one, with every mark and scratch imitated to perfection.

"Any more questions before you go out to break? Right, then. You may go—apart from those who have their English to do again."

Alex, for once not being one of those, filed out with the rest. Out in the playground, he stood for a moment uncertain. He still had hopes of getting someone to join him in foiling Mrs Thoroughgood's plot, and at the moment Brenda remained the best bet, but she'd have to be handled carefully.

She was over the far side of the playground, giggling (as always) in the middle of a group of her friends. Alex went over to the tuckshop and bought a bag of crisps. Then he walked slowly across and deliberately past her group, opening the packet and cramming the largest crisp into his mouth. He kept his mouth wide open, timing the first real crunch for when he was closest to Brenda.

He had not miscalculated. Brenda quit her group at once, and appeared at his side. She reached into his packet and came out with a huge handful—very nearly half.

"Why do you think Mrs T. wants us to go and watch the Prime Minister?" he asked, while she chomped away.

"Search me." She shrugged. "Better than doing Maths or something, isn't it?" She reached out again, but Alex managed to move, so that her hand missed the bag without it seeming to be his fault.

"Suppose I told you that I'm pretty certain she's aiming to kill the Prime Minister?"

Brenda suddenly wheeled round in front of him, stopping him dead. She put both hands on her hips.

"And suppose I tell *you* you're the stupidest boy that ever lived. Your head's so full of your crazy stories, you don't know what's real and what isn't. Why on earth should she? I mean, even supposing she was the greatest criminal in the world—like you keep saying she is—what good could it possibly do her to murder the Prime Minister?"

"They do," Alex argued earnestly. "They do things like that. I've seen it on scores of films and videos and that."

"Films! Videos! This isn't a film or a video. She's our class teacher, in a very ordinary school. And even if she did want to, *how* could she do it?"

"With her umbrella. She's got..."

"With her umbrella! Now I've heard it all!"

She snatched the remainder of the bag of crisps out of his hand before he had time to think, and marched off back to her friends, cramming the last few crisps in as she went, so she wouldn't have to offer any.

Alex gave up. He despairingly surveyed the playground once more, his eyes resting for a moment on Phil, who was belting away at the tennis ball that was all they were allowed for breaktime football. No, Phil was out of the question, and there just wasn't anyone else he liked or trusted that he hadn't already offended by ditching them. How in the world had he managed to lose his grip over the class like this?

Whatever the reason, it was quite clear that he was in this alone, and he'd have to remain alone.

X

The day of the visit was one of those really superb ones that often comes in late May—an absolutely cloudless sky, and a sun with enough power to make you wonder whether even to take a sweater to school, let alone an anorak. What with the weather and the coming trip out, Mrs Thoroughgood's class was so restless in the morning that even she had difficulty in controlling it. Alex, sitting tense and rigid, with his stomach a tight knot, couldn't help noticing that she threatened extra work, staying behind after school, and vague, menacing punishments to various individuals. But not once did she threaten to cancel the excursion.

When the class went out for break, he hung about in the classroom, hoping to get a closer look at the umbrella, there in its usual place at the end of the radiator. He was almost within reach of it when Mrs

Thoroughgood suddenly raised her head from sorting out papers on her desk.

"Alex! Outside. What are you doing, hanging around in here on a day like this?"

He moved reluctantly towards the door. She was clever, and she was cool. Fancy bringing an umbrella to school on a day like this! And just parking it in its usual place. Yet she must be almost as nervous as he was. He spent the rest of the long break wandering unhappily back and forth, past the classroom window, but he didn't dare to try and get in again.

Just as the whistle went for the end of break, a surprising thing happened. A huge, grey car—a Mercedes—drove slowly through the school gates and swung round into the teachers' car park. There were excited whispers on all sides.

"Who's that?"

"Who's that?"

"Wow! What a car!"

Alex knew who it would be. He hung
back from going in for a moment, just to
make certain, and sure enough, the bald
head of Villansky appeared over the top of
the car door. Villansky walked over to the
main door of the school, and stood there
waiting, while Alex went on in.

He and his class were brought out again almost immediately to be lined up on the front playground along with the rest of the school. The younger juniors moved off first, and Alex noted that each class teacher walked about two-thirds of the way down the column. In spite of accusations of pushing in, he managed to get himself in that position in his own class line. The only really embarrassing thing about that was that he turned out to be next to Phil and immediately behind Brenda, both of whom obviously thought he'd tried to get in there so as to make up to them.

He had to put up with that. They would see.

Meanwhile, Mrs Thoroughgood was calmly chatting with Villansky over by the front door. Again Alex marvelled at her coolness. To be talking so openly to him. Presumably she'd made up some story to explain his presence to the other teachers.

Had she also explained why she was carrying her umbrella under this hot sun?

Eventually the order to move came. Alex had calculated his position in the line to perfection, and Mrs Thoroughgood, with Villansky beside her, was walking so close to him that if he'd wanted, he could have reached out and snatched the umbrella off her.

XI

Even after the arrival of the whole school, the pavements along each side of the main road were only lined about two deep. Behind those who were waiting, there were people going about their normal shopping, or whatever. A few kids seemed to have brought little Union Jacks to wave, there were policemen spaced along the road in front of the onlookers—one every thirty metres or so—but otherwise no great excitement or enthusiasm.

Alex's main fear had been that once the class was safely in position, Mrs Thoroughgood might move to another part of it. But she didn't. She was right there beside him. She was even holding Villansky's arm now! On the far side of Villansky was Brenda. Alex could hear her outbursts of laughter clearly and often, but Mrs Thoroughgood and Villansky were talking so intimately together that it was impossible to catch a single word. On Alex's other side was Phil.

"What's up, Alex?" Phil asked. "You're very quiet. Surely you've got some fancy story about this little lot."

He sounded friendly, but Alex couldn't answer him. "Oh, by the way," Phil went on, "talking of fancy stories, little John Jones is going to be back at school next week. You know—little 'dead' John Jones? So he isn't dead, but apparently he's been really, really ill."

"Who told you?" Alex's voice was harsh with tension and suspicion.

"Mum did. She's got to know his mum quite well. He's had rheumatic fever or something like that."

Whatever Alex might have had to say in answer to that was interrupted by an exchange on his other side. Miss Smalley had come to Mrs Thoroughgood with a message from the Head.

"She says, could you lead with your class on the way back please, Mrs Thoroughgood."

"Yes, of course. Oh, by the way, I don't think you've met my husband, have you? He's being really wicked taking an hour off work because he says he's seen just about every high-up in the country except the Prime Minister, and he wanted a peek. What's more, he says he's going to miss a two-million-pound contract just through being here instead of there. Tom, this is Anne Smalley."

"Don't mind her, Miss Smalley," said the bald-headed man, shaking hands. "She's exaggerating as usual. It's only a *one*-million-pound contract." He laughed at his own joke. His accent was flat, northern English, not in the least foreign.

"Oh!" Miss Smalley was quite flustered. "I'm awfully pleased to meet you. We hear such a lot about you—she's always boasting."

Alex only smiled grimly to himself. Just his luck to have his brilliant game shattered on both sides, right at the most exciting bit. He didn't know how much further he'd have dared to follow it through, but just a *little* further . . .

Everyone was suddenly craning forward. Far off, down the road, there were dazzling flashes of sun on chrome and glass, and all around a chatter of excitement. A single police motorbike came past. Then a police car. Six more motorbikes, three abreast. Then three huge, black limousines, the middle one with a little flag fluttering at the front, a ripple of cheering and flag-waving accompanying it up each side of the road.

Alex heard an agonised wail from Brenda. "Which one *is* it? I don't know which is the Prime Minister!"

"That one. There." Mrs Thoroughgood raised her umbrella and pointed.

The day's tension burst in Alex at the same time as the cheers around him. His right hand shot out, knocking the point of the umbrella high in the air. He knew, he *knew* that a tiny pphtt! sound was drowned out by the noise around. He knew that a shot had gone harmlessly into the air, way over the houses opposite, to drop to earth miles off.

Of course there would be a lot of heavy music to face now. Even as the ripple of cheering died down, the last of the police bikes passed, and people began to leave, Mrs Thoroughgood was rounding furiously on him.

"What in heaven's name did you do that for? You absurd little boy."

Anything, anything but the truth could be said. "I'm sorry, Mrs Thoroughgood. I got pushed and I was slipping off the kerb, and I grabbed at your umbrella to stop myself. I'm very sorry."

"It didn't feel as if you were grabbing. Much more like . . ."

"Typical, isn't it?" Mr Thoroughgood interrupted good-humouredly. "You wait all that time for something, and when it happens, you blink and miss it. Still, young man, in spite of your attempted diversion, *I* didn't miss it."

"Well I did—most of it," Mrs Thoroughgood snapped. She really was quite terrifyingly cross.

"Ah, what a shame," soothed her husband. "I'll bet this lad did too, didn't you?"

"Yes," said Alex.

"That's punishment enough, surely."

"Just remind me," Mrs Thoroughgood said bitingly, "never to stand near you ever again, Alex. Right, class! Back to the school!"

On the way, Brenda managed to get next to him instead of Phil. Her eyes were round with wonderment.

"Gosh, Alex. You really believed it, didn't you?"

The worst was now over, and Alex could answer quite casually. "Not really. But it wasn't worth taking the risk. I had to do something, even if there was only the titchiest chance it might be true."

"But there wasn't even the titchiest chance, was there?"

"No, I suppose not." Alex grinned a bit sheepishly.

"Wow, Alex. You're stupid, but you really are brave. Mrs T.'s face was really something when you bashed her brolly!"

Brenda began to giggle, and she giggled her way right back into the classroom. Even after the lesson started, an occasional snort could be heard coming from her direction.

XII

That evening, Mrs Thoroughgood lay slumped over her console with her head cradled in her arms. Villansky hovered anxiously near, not daring to speak. Eventually she raised her head and stared at him viciously.

"The one job you had to do, Villansky—keep that blasted kid in check.

But could you do it? Oh, no. It was too much for you. You had to be so thrilled at being allowed to pass yourself off as my husband that you were incapable of doing a pitifully simple job. As if I'd ever have *you* as a husband—a big, bald, bloated worm like you!"

"I did my best, Mrs Thoroughgood," whined Villansky. "He was just too quick for me. I didn't think he was going to move at all. Then he did."

"He's always too quick. He's got to be got rid of and that's that. I'll just have to handle any suspicion that comes my way, but at least *he* won't be there to stir it up. And this is another job I'm not trusting you with. Give me good, fast robots any day."

She turned back to her gigantic keyboard and began stabbing frenziedly at key after key, programming the robots to attend to the immediate disposal of Alex.

XIII

In his bedroom, Alex stared hard and thoughtfully at the warm-air central heating vent he knew concealed Mrs Thoroughgood's spy-camera. He winked at it, then went over to the window.

The robots would be arriving soon. He wasn't sure how they'd arrive, nor how he'd fight them off, but he'd be too quick for them as well. She'd see!